The Bare Naked Book

Words by
Kathy Stinson

Pictures by
Melissa Cho

annick press
toronto • berkeley

Bodies, bodies!
Big and small,
short and tall,
young and old—

Every BODY is different!

Hair

Dripping,
braided,
curly,
straight,

on heads and faces
and other places.

Where is
your hair?

Eyes that see and eyes that are blind.

Crying, winking.
Where are your eyes?

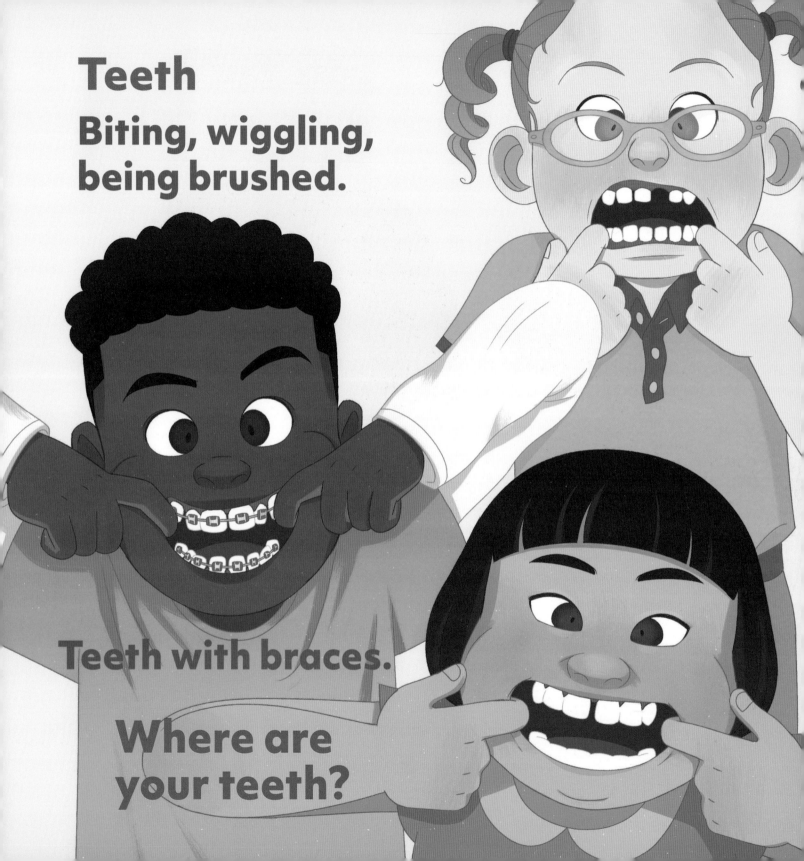

Teeth
Biting, wiggling, being brushed.

Teeth with braces.

Where are your teeth?

Tongues
Licking, slurping, candy-colored.

Can *you* see *yours*?

Where is your tongue?

Shoulders

Hiding in a gown.
Riding shoulders,
up and down.

Where are your shoulders?

Arms
Swimming, brimming,
swinging, flinging,

Hands

Washing, holding, clapping, folding, dining, signing.

Where are your hands?

Fingers

Squeezing,
poking,
getting pinched,
and making music.

Where are your fingers?

Chests and breasts
With hair, with milk,
and nipples like buttons.

Where are
your nipples?

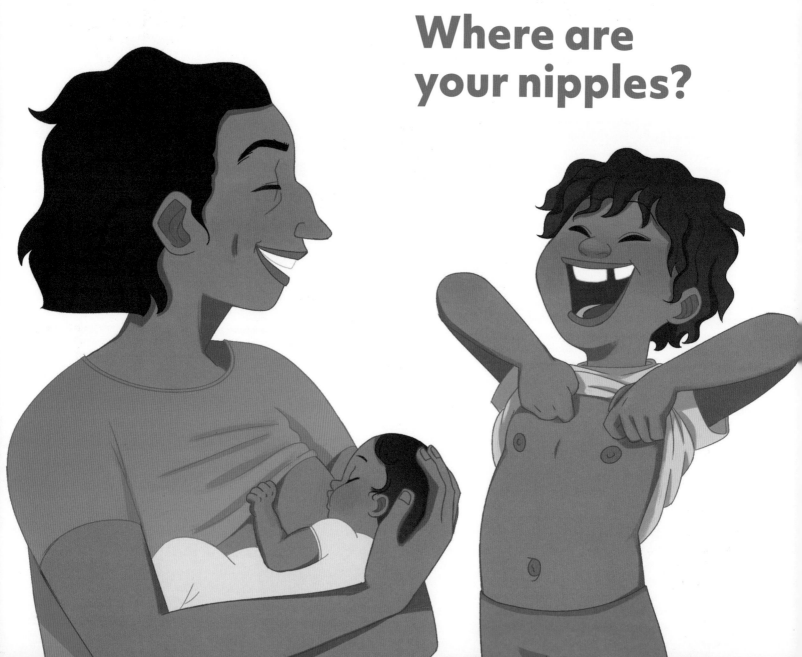

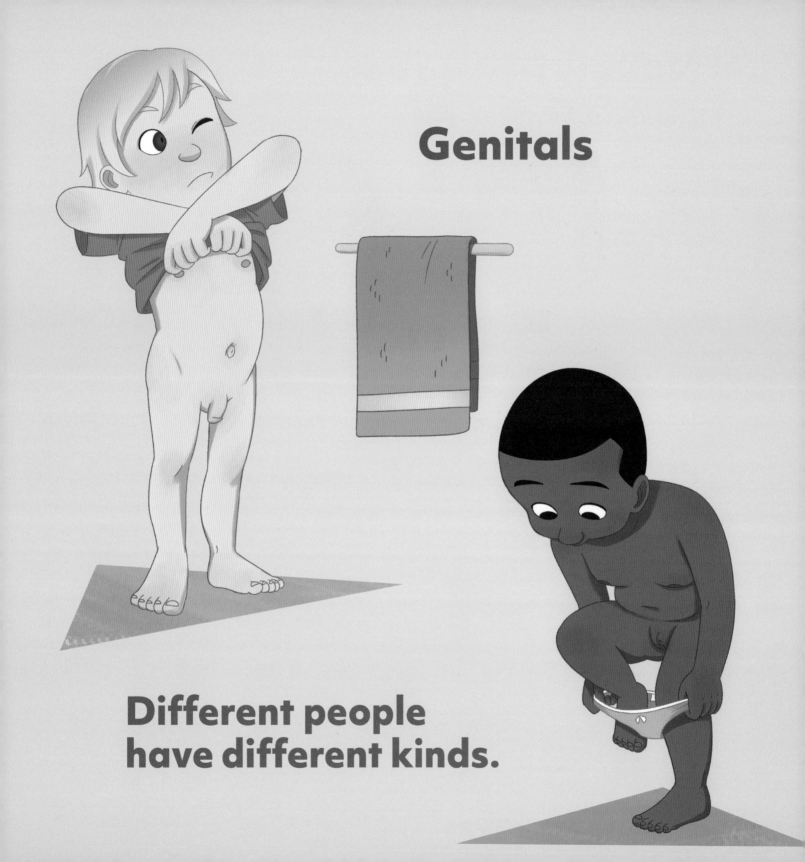

Genitals

Different people have different kinds.

Whatever you call whatever *you* have, your genitals belong to you.

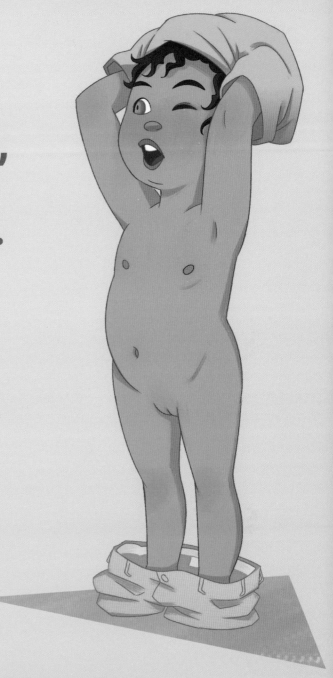

Where are your genitals?

Bums
Standing up,
    sitting down.

Remember please to wipe—
and wash your hands!

Where is your bum?

Knees

Together, apart.
With a scrape, yeow!
Coming and going.
All better now.

Where are your knees?

Feet

Stamping, hopping, tiptoeing, stomping.

Where are your feet?

Toes

Rainbow, yummy, squishy, splashy.

Which-little-piggy?

Where are your toes?

Where is
your skin?

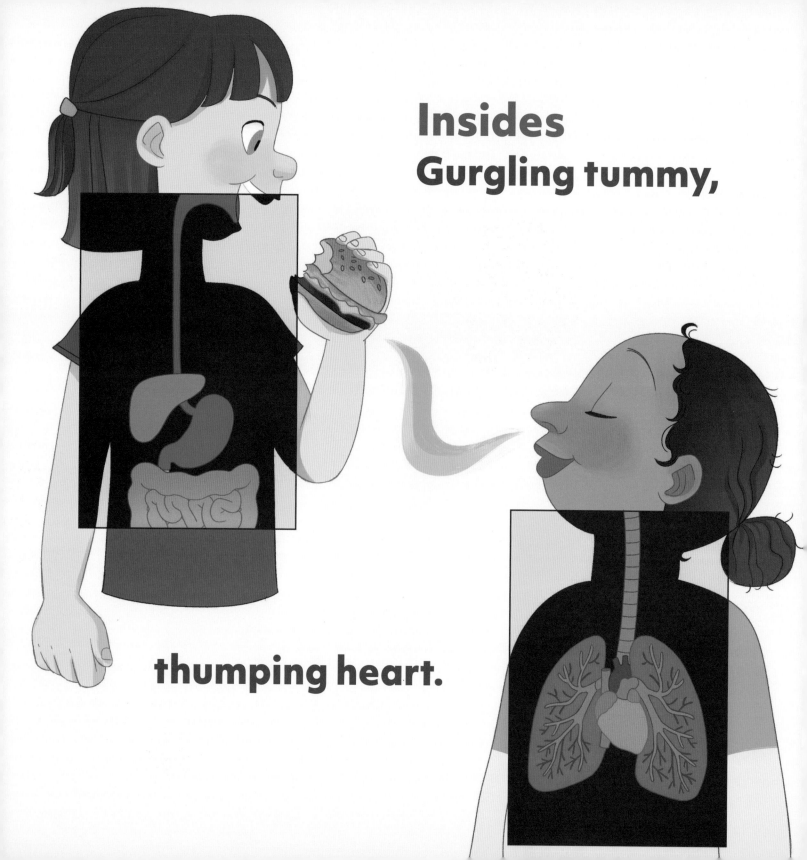

Insides
Gurgling tummy,
thumping heart.

Where happy and sad live under every part.

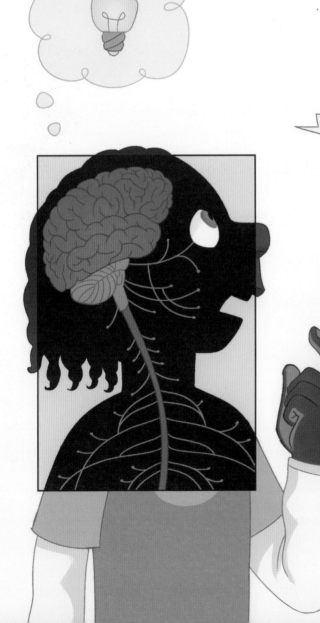

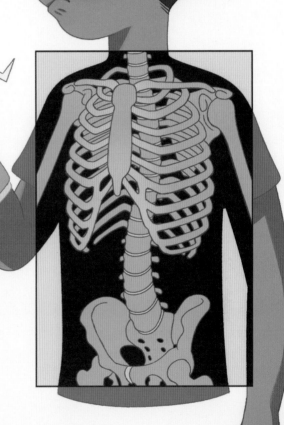

Where are your insides?

Bodies, bodies
To love and to celebrate.

So many wonderful bodies!

A Note from the Author

The original publication of *The Bare Naked Book* in 1986 caused quite a stir. It was considered pretty daring at the time to show naked bodies and talk about them frankly in a children's book! But we knew it was important for children to see different bodies being celebrated and to learn about their own. The book was fun, matter-of-fact, and often appeared on lists of recommended titles related to themes of body image and personal safety.

Over the years, conversations around diversity and identity evolved significantly. We began to realize that too many children would not find themselves and important people in their lives within the book's pages. Annick Press and I agreed it was time for an update. We worked closely with equity educator and consultant j wallace skelton to reimagine the book for today's readers.

Showing a fuller range of human beings and their bodies required new illustrations, and happy was the day artist Melissa Cho came on board. We also made significant changes to the text. For example, rather than specifying "penis" and "vagina," as we did originally, and assigning them rigidly to males and females, this time we have used simply "genitals," leaving adult readers free to talk with children about variations in gender identity and genitalia, and the words they might prefer to use to refer to them. Having a shared understanding of the terms a child uses for their genitals helps in recognizing and intervening in cases of sexual abuse while also letting each child choose how they self-identify.

Whether you're a parent, caregiver, educator, or counselor, we hope that you and the children in your lives will delight in finding yourselves in this new and improved *bare naked* celebration of bodies!

Kathy Stinson

Kathy Stinson is the award-winning author of more than thirty books for young people. She lives in Rockwood, Ontario.

Melissa Cho is a designer and illustrator working in children's media. She lives in Southern Ontario.

j wallace skelton is a trans person, an equity and justice consultant, and a professor of Queer Studies in Education. j hopes you find people in this book that remind you how great you are. Really.

We acknowledge the support of the Canada Council for the Arts and the Ontario Arts Council, and the participation of the Government of Canada/la participation du gouvernement du Canada for our publishing activities.

Library and Archives Canada Cataloguing in Publication

Title: The bare naked book / words by Kathy Stinson ; pictures by Melissa Cho.
Names: Stinson, Kathy, author. | Cho, Melissa, illustrator.
Description: Revised edition. | Previous editions illustrated by Heather Collins.
Identifiers: Canadiana (print) 20200327275 | Canadiana (ebook) 20200327283 | ISBN 9781773214726 (hardcover) | ISBN 9781773214740 (HTML) | ISBN 9781773214757 (PDF) | ISBN 9781773214764 (Kindle)
Subjects: LCSH: Human body–Juvenile literature. | LCSH: Gender identity–Juvenile literature.
Classification: LCC QM27 .S75 2021 | DDC j611–dc23

Library and Archives Canada Cataloguing in Publication

Title: The bare naked book / words by Kathy Stinson ; pictures by Melissa Cho.
Names: Stinson, Kathy, author. | Cho, Melissa, illustrator.
Description: Previous editions illustrated by Heather Collins.
Identifiers: Canadiana 20220419418 | ISBN 9781773214733 (softcover)
Subjects: LCSH: Human body–Juvenile literature. | LCSH: Gender identity–Juvenile literature. | LCSH: Individual differences–Juvenile literature. | LCGFT: Instructional and educational works. | LCGFT: Picture books.
Classification: LCC QM27 .S75 2023 | DDC j611–dc23

Published in the U.S.A. by Annick Press (U.S.) Ltd.
Distributed in Canada by University of Toronto Press.
Distributed in the U.S.A. by Publishers Group West.

Printed in China

annickpress.com
kathystinson.com
melissacho.net

Also available as an e-book. Please visit annickpress.com/ebooks for more details.